Spring Break at Pokeweed Public School

by John Bianchi

Even though we all love our winter hockey games, toboggan rides and snowball fights, the gang at Pokeweed Public School is always happy to see the first signs of spring.

We are constantly on the lookout for:
New buds on the big maple tree in front of the school.

Tulips popping up in the flowerbed around the flagpole.

POP!

POP!

POP!

POP!

POP!

Canada geese honking their way north in a big "V".

HONK! HONK!

HONK!

And April showers that wash away
the last islands of crusty snow.

Every year, we celebrate the arrival of spring with a playground cleanup, parent-teacher interviews and a visit from a famous author.

But the event that everyone loves the most is Pokeweed Public School's annual Spring Break Camp-Out.

Can I go, Mom? Please, Please, please, please,
Attention Parents
We will once again be holding our annual Spring Break Camp-Out. All those students wishing to attend should report to the school parking lot no later than 8 a.m. WITH ONLY THE BARE ESSENTIALS NEEDED TO SURVIVE A NIGHT IN THE WILDERNESS.
Student's name
Will ☐ Will not ☐ Attend.
Parent's signature
Thank you for your support.
Principal Slugmeyer

This year, as always, we neatly packed a few odds and ends and gathered in the school parking lot. Then, under the expert supervision of Ms. Mudwortz and Principal Slugmeyer, we all boarded the bus and headed off for . . .

. . . Lake Weegonnahaha, the best campground in the whole wide world.

At the campsite, some of us had a few problems setting up our tents. But with a little help and encouragement from good old Ms. Mudwortz, everyone got set up and moved in just fine.

After lunch, Principal Slugmeyer took us down to the lake for a lesson in fly casting. He made it look so easy! Then it was our turn, and on the count of "three," we all cast together.

I think we could have gotten better at it, but we only had one chance.

After dinner, Billy showed us why you should never stand up in a canoe. Then Ms. Mudwortz taught us how to make "s'mores." They taste so good, everyone always wants some more! Especially Principal Slugmeyer. He just kept eating s'more and s'more and s'more and s'more!

THE ULTIMATE S'MORE

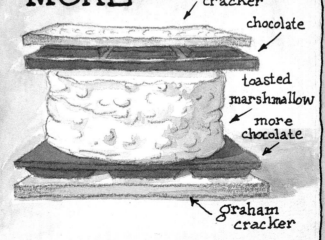

graham cracker

chocolate

toasted marshmallow

more chocolate

graham cracker

Students:

Hopefully, during our visit to lake Weegonnahaha, we will have an opportunity to make s'mores. You may want to memorize these instructions.

Sincerely,
Ms. Mudwortz

① Stack ingredients in the order shown.
② Eat.
③ For a s'more "melt," place near fire until soft and gooey.

As we sat around the fire, Principal Slugmeyer spoke about the legend of Ogopokeweed. It seems that although there have been many sightings of this secretive creature, no one has ever taken a picture of it. Ms. Mudwortz explained that cryptozoologists are scientists who hunt for mysterious animals and that even they have been unable to prove Ogopokeweed exists.

When the fire began to die out, Principal Slugmeyer warned us that Ogopokeweed was known to have a humungous appetite. The wise campers of Lake Weegonnahaha always store their food high up in the trees. So on the way back to our tents, we put all the leftover snacks into a big pack and tied it to a sturdy branch.

As we lay in our sleeping bags listening to the cries of the loons on the lake, Melody and I talked about Ogopokeweed and imagined what it would be like to be cryptozoologists. And that's when we got the idea: *We* would solve the mystery of Lake Weegonnahaha ourselves.

After everyone was asleep, we slipped outside and set up my instant camera so that if anything tried to get at the food pack, the camera would take a picture. Then we hopped back into our tent, snuggled down into our sleeping bags and fell fast asleep.

Later, we were awakened by something rustling around outside. I was so scared, I jumped into Melody's sleeping bag with her. Then we saw the flash of the camera and heard something go crashing off into the bushes. We were so afraid that we just stayed in that big old sleeping bag the whoooooole night!

The next morning, we crawled out of our tent and looked around. It sure seemed as if Ogopokeweed had paid us a visit — the pack was wide open, and there was food all over. But the picture was a big disappointment. We wanted to continue our investigation, but unfortunately, it was time for us to clean up the campsite and head for home.

On the bus, Melody and I told Ms. Mudwortz that we had decided to become famous cryptozoologists someday. She thought that was a great idea. When we showed her our picture, she pointed out that although we had missed the mysterious creature's head, we still had an important clue to the Ogopokeweed puzzle. Whatever the monster looked like, it seemed to be wearing a hat just like Principal Slugmeyer's!